Vires

Vires
Cloak of Dawn/Silent Voice
Vol. 2

by

Ngozi Patience Umajie

Ngozi Patience Umajie

Landover, Maryland

Dedication

This book is dedicated to my two wonderful sons, Joseph and Elems Junior and also to my late parents. Late Chief G.W.Umajie and Mrs. Selina Ugbe-Umajie.

Table of contents

Biography

This book is all about poetry that came from the mind of an immigrant lady, who migrated to the United States of America, from a tribe called Ekpeye in the Ahoada local government area of the Rivers State Nigeria in West Africa in the early 1990s. Nigeria was commonly referred to as the Giant of Africa during her oil-boom days. Nigeria truly was a giant nation to her, as far as Life as a girl, boy, man or woman is concerned. The reality of life as she saw it was more than just being a daughter, wife and then mother. Her dream as a kid from a village called Oshiugbokor village growing up was to one day visit the lighted town, where there was something called electricity. That city then was Ahoada, which she actually visited at the age of eight with her mother Selina Ugbe-Umajie, born in Ogbo in Ekpeye village as well. She never stopped dreaming of the bigger world around her until she met the man of her dreams — or so she thought. In the mid-80s Elems Felix Ukwu Sr., promised to take her to the paradise of the world she imagined. Paradise then turned into Hades, but for the Mercy and Grace of God Almighty. Blessed with two wonderful sons, she raised them as a single mother thereafter. She decided to put most of her life, culture, community, and the world around her into poetry form. She currently has her two surviving sisters and two brothers with their families all in Nigeria. Her Father passed on in 2007 while her mother passed on in 2012.

In this book you will not only read the poet's language, which sometimes makes no sense to the ordinary mind, but you will be given the opportunity to understand what the poet's message is all about in her own words.

Introduction

Vires in our micro and macro world. The unjust, superseding the just in our complex world.

Therefore, there is a need for humanity to curb the vires in our societies by calling a spade what it is. A need to get involved and not look the other way. This is viewed through a poetic lens. The need to search ourselves and address the injustice of man towards our fellow man is a vital issue in our society. The power that another possesses over his fellow man, "Lording" over another must be addressed. For instance, a husband, who for the fact that he helped his wife migrate from Africa to the United States of America, or anybody for that matter, assumes that his so-called wife, husband, friend or relatives are bound to a life of servitude because he was instrumental to their migration, is absurd. One individual telling another, "as long as I am footing the bill, whatever I demand of you has to be done" is one example of many vires our society must get rid of. Imagine a husband, telling his wife, "as long as you're my wife, and I'm feeding you, whenever I want "it", you have to give "it". Imagine being, A slave to circumstance. Imagine a husband refusing to give his wife a ride to an appointment because she refused to give him, "you know what." Why would any sane person give themselves up to anyone that treats them like a perpetual slave? Why in the world would one individual or group of individuals think that they are better than the other? After all, if we believe that we are all created in God's image, God our supernatural creator, and we attest to that, why then should a man have absolute dominion over another man? Why would anyone be seen or treated less than the other even in their micro family? How about being abused by a group of individuals just because you are a foreigner living in a foreign land, is that right? They exploit you financially and so many other ways, knowing that you will not have the guts to pursue them legally because of your status. These, and others were the reason why this book is written from a poetic mind. Vires in our micro and macro society will be pointed out by the author in this book in an effort for a better and greater life in our society for all humans, no matter the environment and situation in which one finds himself/herself. There is a need for every "girl, lady, boy or man" to be treated just like the rest of humanity. Every person needs to be treated with dignity and respect. Respect they say, is give and take. How do you expect to receive when you fail to give? The world today is chaotic because of the other man seeing his fellow man as less than a human being. The powerful and rich ought not to step on the poor and Lord over them just because they have their wealth. Nations try to control other nations because they can. How can we obtain peace and tranquility in a world where a group of individuals are treated in a way, that if put in that same position, the adversary would not be able to stomach such treatment? They would not be able to stand being on the receiving end of the powers. As it was said in the Golden Rule and similarly stated in Matthew 7:12 and Luke 6:31, "Do unto others as you would have them do unto you." The most outrageous of the vires, even in our so-called civilized world, is the treatment that is dished to certain foreigners by a few individuals simply because one migrated from another part of the world than another. These few individuals forgot that the earth is the Lord's and the fullness thereof and they that dwell therein; as it is written in 1 Corinthians 10:26 and Psalms 24:1. Exodus 23:9-12 tells us, "not to oppress a stranger," yet we do it anyways, and still claim to be a God-fearing people.

Conclusively therefore, this book is bringing home to us the need to search ourselves and the community around us to make sure we do everything within our power to make the world a better place for all, no matter their affiliations. Speak up against evil when you notice or observe it. Do not look the other way or keep silence. Let us make the world a better place for all. After all, none of us will live on this planet earth forever.

Vires: Cloak of Dawn/Silent Voice

Micro vires

The world is created by God to all that believe. Though, a few may say in their hearts there is no God; but with every indication in our human hemisphere, only the fools would state there is no God just like it was stated in the Holy Bible. In the book of Psalms. 14:1.
We may then wonder why all the confusions and heartache in the ways man is viewed culturally as it starts in every homes and communities.

I seriously wonder and perplexed to the max, based on the culture I was birth from. A child is hardly allowed to speak especially in the gathering of the elders, the worst is a woman not allowed to speak even within the family gathering just because one is born with a different genitals than that of a male born.

As a kid I could not fathom the practice whereby you cannot express yourself before the elders. As a child you are not allowed to speak or as an adult woman either, no speaking by a woman during a family meeting because you are a woman unless your male sibling had to speak on your behalf. There is no ifs and buts as
long as this practice is concerned in the tribe I was birth at, and I am sure that there were others that felt the same way like I did but had no way of speaking and protesting against it.

This culture is absurd and detrimental to the development of any woman or girl as one who possesses God-given potentials are being hindered and damaged by the society looking at a group of individuals as less that human beings. This primitive and unfounded notion of women being less than a man had to be stopped. Every child should have a say in her home even though one is born a woman. A woman should not be seen just like a sex object and a baby-making factory.

My intention is to bring this to the broader light so that parents, leaders and men would allow every human beings express themselves as humans and not to lord over others because of their cultural stipulations of those autocratic individuals that lived before us and their intent to control others for their own greed. This primitive barbaric culture toward women who are the weaker sex by nature should be done with. How would a girl be deprived of her father's home because she is not married or stay married in a loveless relationship? This to a Western person or woman may sound obscure but for an African, a Nigerian and an Ekpeye woman from Osiugbokor, it is very real, and it is still going on today in the 21st century. This is devastating to an articulate person and our culture needs to be inclusive of every gender, either tall or short, rich or poor, beautiful or ugly, and especially female or male. We are all human, and we should be treated with equal respect. Beauty although, is in the eye of the beholder.

 Respect, they say is "give and take".

A young girl is given out for marriage while the male siblings are sent to high schools and colleges. A so-called wife is verbally, emotionally, and physically abused in every way possible and still remains a wife by producing babies. When the babies are not produced, the woman is shamed, not the man. A wife's attempt to leave such union is frowned upon. She is considered an outcast and a shame to her parents and family. My hope is that someday soon these injustices toward women, such as the circumcision of female genital "Clitoris", would be a thing of the past.

The men could have sex with whomever and whenever with no regards to their marital status; but let the woman attempt such an act in any minute way, and her life will be in danger as she is beaten to a pulp and humiliated in all manner of degradation, if not killed. Could you imagine a culture that makes a woman return a dowry paid on her head during traditional marriage ceremony because she chooses to leave an abusive marriage even after all the pain she had gone through, as a result of child bearing and all other disfigurations?

This to me is absurd, and I am certain no man would want this for themselves if this situation is reversed. These types of practices in our society, especially in my tribe and the world around us, must be addressed. All humans should be treated with equal respect and dignity no matter their gender, religious affiliations or ethnicity. These vires in our micro communities need to be addressed. We do not need to look the other way, and to achieve this positive change both the men and women need to get involved to make all life worth living.

No matter the gender, shape or shades, we are all humans. Don't dish your neighbor the food that you know you cannot eat; Just saying.

The Bitter Truth

Who amongst us would say that the truth does not matter? There is a popular saying that goes, "the truth shall set you free." What a myth! No one is against the truth, but with the look of things the truth hurts. You may hear all of that mumble jumble, but as you read you will adhere with my title, as it is stated above, The Bitter Truth.

The truth is bitter in every aspect of life except in the spiritual arena. The truth is only emphasized consciously or unconsciously when it involves the truly practical Christians. This, even in our present generation or within any arena you find yourself and others, is far-fetched. These days you can hardly tell the difference; as the assumed believers sometimes cannot be differentiated from the unbelievers, as their words cannot be digested as well.

You may wonder why the truth is bitter, but with my investigative intuitions and the endowment of nature, what you would hear is "everybody lies." You may think it is just a slogan, but in reality, it is practical in our society, because the truth will not only hurt you, but it will isolate you. It will isolate one amongst his/her peers, at workplaces, in the church, in the clubs, and in all walks of life. Sometimes, the truth hinders your success in life. One then wonders why it is generally stated that "the truth will set you free." It sounds and appears as if this well-known quote is not a fact of life in the outward sense of it, but when considering one's spiritual and personal freedom, the truth actually will set you free. Especially in this society were lies is the norm of the day from the top to the least amongst us. The United States of America, of course, the civilized world that is filled with men and women from all works of the universe. Therefore as in one woman's opinion, I am assuming that the freedom of telling the truth is spiritual in terms of you and your creator, if you believe in the supernatural relationship with God. But for man and our society, telling the truth is bitter as you are seen as a dumb and stupid individual. One is labelled as the all-knowing, all righteous. You may wonder why she is saying all this. But it is generally stated also, "that the proof of the pudding is in the eating."

This is my personal experiences, and I very much believe that someone out there would relate to this. You ask a fellow Christian a simple but a direct question, either they look at your face and lie or they get angry with you and tell you to stay out of their business or they tell you don't judge. Why am I judging if all I want to know is the truth of a rumor, which I don't want to be part off. In 1 John 4:6, we are from God, and whosoever knows God listens to us but whoever is not from God does not listen to us. This is how we recognize the Spirit of truth and the spirit of falsehood. There are so many references in the scripture as believers that speaks to us about the truth. In Ephesians 6:14: "Stand firm then, with the belt of truth buckled around your waist, with the breastplate of righteousness in place/" Also Exodus 20:16: "You shall not give false testimony against your neighbor," but these days even the so-called believers indulge themselves in these small lies as they call it" which they thinks it is okay." If okay, then what is the difference between nonbelievers and believers in terms of our Christian faith?

Vires: Cloak of Dawn/Silent Voice

Therefore, I am now beginning to believe that everybody lies. You try to live by the truth and you see yourself not progressing. Those that lie seem to get to the top randomly. The society seem to accept them and adore them with their false testimonies. You stand to state the truth, you become the villain amongst your fellow believers. Why can't I live to attest to my faith having known the truth? As a result of your truth, even amongst your peers, you are then treated as an outsider. Why is it so? Should it be because our society has turned against God and focused its attention on materialism, or is it the signs of the end of time? Or should it be that people don't care about the truth anymore?

A young man and woman who profess to be children of God, already married, their partners either at home or native countries, go and marry another, all in the name of American green card. Still they call themselves Christian, Holy Ghost filled, and they appeared and stare at you as though you are the one that is not doing something right. It is obviously indicative in this Western society that success in this our modern-day miniature of Sodom and Gomorrah cannot be achieved as a practical Christian as years is taken out of your life for practicing what you preach and believe. Anyway; why would I feel this way after all. The Bible tells us about Abraham in a foreign land denying his wife Sarah, claiming she was the sister, which means these individuals are doing what they needed to do in the name of survival. If that is acceptable, why do we then say that liars cannot make it to Heaven? Should there be an exception then? Why is the human life so complicated? You say one and do the other. Should it be "do as I say but not as I do"?

In a work environment, there appears a kind of code of silence. You see the individual doing the wrong thing. Everyone around pretends as if they do not see what is going on because they don't want to lose their job, especially at this difficult time whereby the chances of getting a job is very slim.

And if you dare speak up, your job is threatened. The bad ones seem to outnumber the good ones. Is this why they say the truth is bitter? Because the bad ones seem to gain more grounds easily.

Even in a relationship, all you see is lies and deceit. You dare not tell all the truth about you to your love ones unless you have not had any skeleton in your cupboard. If you do, your relationship is over. What a world of deceit and lies, the truth be told, there is no one without a skeleton in their cupboard. It could be why the Bible also tells us that blessed are those that their sins are covered. Psalm 32:1.

You work in an establishment. You are written up for something that never happened, and you were advised by your boss not to follow it up for reasons best known to them. What a code of silence?

Who is telling the truth then, as man lives in the fear of the unknown in the land of many, just to survive by living a life of lies and pretense, in a society where lies is the order of the day. Whereby, a straight and honest individual is deemed stupid. Ponder on this as you read,

Although, it is said there is no one righteous but Christ, why do we then pretend to be what we are not? Giving false testimonies to gain notoriety in a church and false tales against your coworkers and lording over your fellow man at work, expecting them not to speak up and if they do, their job is on the line? This is happening every day in our society. The truth they say is bitter, but someone had to tell it. Thanks.

Vires: Cloak of Dawn/Silent Voice

Macro vires

The poetic justice of our past and present human existence is so prominent and appears inanimate in our being. Though, vires as defined in Latin as powers. Powers could be demonstrated, used in different levels and categories in our human existence. An example of Vires is having the authority to tell a person what action they must take. This and several actions starts from our homes, communities, and the world around us and those around us. An example of vires is an action that is beyond the powers as detailed in the law, ultra vires. Having the authority to tell a person what action they must take, intra vires. One would not overlook the fact that power is in existence and operative in every aspect of our daily lives.

The beauty and the gloominess of it is dependent on those that truly exhibit the powers. Power could be very domineering in the sense that if not checked, it could be destructive to our human existence.

It could be positively used for the progress of the home, community or the world at large. It could be negatively exercised that could be detrimental to everyone, even those that use them. It is very enticing to all that pursue it for one reason or the other, but the truth of the matter is that it has to be checked in every level. This is my main reason of bringing it to people's awareness as it pertains to my personal experiences and observations in a broader perspective. This would be buttressed further as I discuss the homes, communities, affiliations,

Vires: Cloak of Dawn/Silent Voice

establishments and the world at large. It is very obvious that the world we live in is corrupt right from the beginning of time, but we are all endowed with power to make the best out of it. There are many within and without, that have not reached out to the glorious salvation power of Christ our redeemer. We assume that if such individuals are endowed with power, their ruler ship could be detrimental to the homes, communities and the world around us. This you would see as it reflects to my poems and more within this text. I am not in any way, shape or form to condemn other beliefs but the only man of peace we all know is Christ, So, as a believer in Him and His teachings, I tend to gear my discussion by using His legacy for the world to emulate. As a professed born-again Christian, I have experienced and done things that does not glorify God Almighty in most of my life, but the fact of the matter is that I tend to hold on to the true meaning of the love of God. No matter how far I wonder away from my belief and testimonies, one thing is for sure in my life, the resurrection power of Christ in me cannot be shot down. So, I tend to speak up with that spirit of boldness wherever I find myself, and for the few that want to lord over another, I appear to be a threat in their domain as they see fit. What would one think of a society where because they think you don't belong you cannot complain about an apartment invested with bedbug? And if you do, there is an allegation against you that you did not pay your rent. You are taken to court even after you have your proof of rent payment. Then after you have proven your case in the court that you paid your rent, they will not stop but will go to any length to make sure you are frustrated to the point of giving up. Human beings are created to love, but there are some bullies out there that is either their way or no way. A lawyer tries to exploit you because they think they own you and because you protested by speaking up and refusing to be exploited. He goes to extra length to make sure he inflicts pain on you one way or the other. What a world of lordship. A boss want to lord over you just because she is on top and you are not, by writing you up for an obvious incident that was not your fault, and for someone who knows her right and speaks up against such act, you now become a target. How about an individual that lives in an apartment for over seven years that never saw a meter that was assigned to her apartment but is being outrageously billed monthly, and when she requests to see her meter from the landlord, she is referred to the electricity supply company, and when she calls the electricity company, she is referred back to the Landlord, and at the point that she became angry realizing that there was something going on, her electricity bills continued to triple and there is nothing she could do because she is being victimized. She is considered a foreigner and who has no judicial privileges. How about an auto insurance company who sold you a comprehensive insurance, and when your car is vandalized they refuse to cover you? How about another refusing to honor a contract you have with them because they see you as an outsider and someone they could victimize and get away with it by saving the company's money, enriching themselves while you suffer because they see you as an outsider? There are a lot of evil and loopholes even in the Western hemisphere that the good people need to look into and to make sure everyone is treated fairly and equally no matter your place of origin as long as you are a human being. This is so unfortunate that people are being victimized on daily bases just because the others feel that they have the upper hand, but the only thing that I as the author of this book is demanding or requesting to the Western world is that there should be a body created to monitor how the different organizations or cooperation deal with the individuals who are seen as outsiders because there are a lot of abuse going on in the society. But my consolation as a writer of this book is that when bad guys are caught, they pay for it in the Western world such as United states of America. It may take time because of their wealth and connections, but the bad guy always pays, if not here, someday beyond this our mother earth. So, I say if you are in a position to stop evil and abuse please act. You may help a fellow live a better life with your actions. To stop the world vires, we must have to stand up against it.

The untold tales of slavery

The prospect of being a slave or slaver is not only in the past but current in our societies and locks into the future of human race.

One would begin to wonder why such an outrageous statement or should it be considered one man's opinion. No not really. It is an obvious understatement by an individual who, without a mix of thought, elaborates on this our present-day's slavery as compared to that of ancient histories.

This text would not be further buttressed upon without first and foremost telling the literal meaning of slavery such as was defined by the American Heritage dictionary, which states that slavery is the condition of being subject or addicted to a specified influence.

In this simple definition, therefore, one could then see the fact that slavery would ever be a thing of the human race as it is present in every aspect of our society even when we tend to frown at that five-lettered word SLAVE. It would never go away. Slavery is present and active in our domestic arenas, in terms of marriages gone wrong, self-imposed as one takes crap from a spouse as a result of low self-esteem, religious boundaries, politically and internationally which one would refer as indirect form of slavery.

What would you say, if an employer would knowingly underpay an employee that is well qualified and skilled less than what actually is appropriate? Then an open slogan that stipulates do not discuss your pay rate with one another. If found doing just that, one is terminated from work. And another individual with less skill and experience is paid more than necessary, fellow men. I would call that an act of slavery. A man is willing to toil profusely to work and pay taxes and abides by every rules and laws of the land but denied almost all privileges as a result of his or her ethnicity. What would you call that? I would call that a form of slavery.

As a believer religiously, I very much see slavery as God's sanctioned. One may see this statement as outrageous, but the truth of the matter is in the general statement that says; in the book of Jeremiah tells us how God's children were in bondage, "simply slavery," and how God sent His prophet to deliver to His people the message of hope, and going through the different chapters, one would not fail to notice that man always suffer as a result of disobedience to God our creator. That even when we disobey, we could as well cry unto Him and He will deliver us, but disobeying God does not go without consequences. And most of the times there is some things to be accomplished as a result of being a slave, and if you go back in history you would agree with me, if you are not a Bible believing person. Why would anyone not believe the word of God anyway? Although, the word said: the fool has said in his heart that there is no God. Why would one say there is no God with all the wonders? Don't be amongst the fool as the Bible states, for indeed there is God. Domestically, slavery is no stranger in most homes, communities, villages and towns. As a girl growing up I observed some act of slavery in my society as the women are treated with little or no respects. A woman cannot speak amongst her kindred just because she is a woman, and if given the opportunity to speak, your brother or uncle had to speak on your behalf or obtain permission on your behalf to enable you to speak. If you don't call that slavery, what else would you call it? Yes, you may call it what you deem necessary. I still will term that slavery as directed towards women. When once an individual freedom is restricted or undermined, we as a community should see that individual as enslaved. Is that how God created Eve for Adam? I thought it was meant to be companionship not sexism? You are married to a man who knows little or nothing about you either by arranged marriage due to the influential nature of your family background or how industrious your family is, and without consent from the young woman, she is given away to marriage, or heaven help you if your groom is brutal. Your marriage becomes a life time of slavery, as you live the rest of your life under the brutality of your husband and his family, unless nature blesses the woman with a male child who grows up to liberate his mother from an abusive relationship. You may wonder how and why? I can't tell you why but how because I grew up with it. The worst is when the woman cannot even run back to her biological family, and if she does, she is sent back to her abusive husband. A man kicks a wife as a football because she catches her husband cheating, and she is beating to pulps. She would still fix food for the husband. Otherwise, she is termed as an untrained woman who wants the man for herself and even called a harlot as such for not wanting to share her husband. If you don't call that slavery what else would you call it? Religiously therefore, a young lady is sexually molested in the name of religion gone bad by a Christian brother, and the woman has no guts to report such incident because you would be seen as the loose one, and in the non-Christian community, the question would be what did she go to his house for? A woman has a baby out of wedlock, she may never be married again by any suitable man but if at all, it had to

Vires: Cloak of Dawn/Silent Voice

be a widower or an old man, but the men can have as many children as they could with multiple sexual partners and the society still embraces them. If that is not a form of slavery, what would you call that? Above is the third world country like the part I came from, but how about the developed countries where most men/women live in fear of being arrested by the law as they were now abused by their so-called partners and wives. A woman goes beyond her boundaries knowing fully well that the man suffers if found guilty of abuse or sexual harassments. This I should say is a form of slavery or a person who thinks he or she would control his partner, by saying "If I can't have you no one should," as in the case of O.J. Simpson and Nicole Brown Simpson. But thank goodness for the developed world as the United States of America, who did not look the other way for such an act of slavery. Who would be the judge? Who actually could say what transpired? Only those that were involved who were the husbands and the wives that are subjected to such a state. Looking from outside in, one would imagine the liberation the deceased felt by bringing another man to the house as per the story of late Nicole Simpson and the agony O.J Simpson felt as a result of his trophy wife, to lay in his bed with another man. Imagine the agony he felt losing his wife, Not just his wife, but his home which was his castle. That he had acquired as a result of his hard earned wealth, which at this time was his mansion and his children. Come to think about it, was slavery gone wrong as the slaved revolted? This may sound over emphasized but O.J felt as a lord over his wife by disrespecting his wife but when she took a stand, it resulted to her untimely death but the joy of it as a woman is that the murderer did not go scot-free like they would usually do in the third world countries.

Vires: Cloak of Dawn/Silent Voice

Some also are self-imposed slavery as the lazy individual decides to stay or live in an abusive relationship because they are lazy to fend for themselves. Slavery has been there then and now and forever. What would you say about a young girl or boy who cannot afford three square meals a day by the parents and is given out for another family as house help and this poor child taken to a city like Port Harcourt or Lagos in Nigeria, whereby the family know little or nothing about his/her living conditions. All they know is that their child has gone to the city for a better life. It only takes a God-fearing man with good heart to do the right thing in such situations. Slavery in our generations, without naming names, I would give an example of a typical illustration of slavery in my home country, Nigeria. In 1993 I had travelled to Lagos for my visa to the United States of America. While in Lagos I had to stay with my then husband's friends' home. Meeting this family for the first time, I discovered that the husband has gone outside the country for military services. This young lady was in Lagos alone with a young daughter about six years old and a son of about four and a young house girl about ten or twelve. I would never forget the images I saw for the few days I stayed with this Nigerian young wife, who was supposedly married to my tribe man but she was from a tribe called Calabar. I spoke to her concerning such treatment but it never made much difference while I was there because she justified the abuse of that poor young girl. The sad thing about such abuse is that the Nigerian society has no law to protect or prevent such wickedness of one man to his fellow man. Why should anyone be subjected to such brutality and Hopelessness? Things are no longer as they were in the 90s, who knows how it was before I got there and how it was after I left? Hopefully, the rich and the privileged would learn not to maltreat the less

Vires: Cloak of Dawn/Silent Voice

fortunate. We as a people can only eradicate slavery and injustice to our fellow man if we stand up against it, God willing.

International slavery

Slavery is a thing of the past I suppose, that would mean that the truth is not told or man had decided to look the other way, hoping because it is not intensely practiced as during the early times up to the time of abolition of slavery. We as a society could leave with it. Non sense, who wants to be a slave if given the option? I very much believe no one. To buttress my point concerning the international slavery, I would first and foremost refer us to the chronological views of slavery and racism in the 16th up to the 18th centuries. The earliest records of slavery, such as the code of Hammurabi, referred to it as an established institution.

Slavery are common amongst hunters and gatherers populations as slaves are dependent on a system of social stratification. Slavery also requires a shortage of labor and a surplus of land to be viable. Therefore, according to David Livingstone, 80,000 Africans died each year before reaching the slave markets of Zanzibar. He said, "To overdraw its evil is a simple impossibility….We passed a slave woman shot or stabbed through the body and lying on the path.[Onlookers] said an Arab who passed early that morning had done it in anger at losing the price he had given for her, because she was unable to walk any longer. We passed a woman tied by the neck to a tree and dead ….We came upon a man dead from starvation …. The strangest disease I have seen in this country seems really to be broken heartedness, and it attacks free men who have been captured and made slaves." Therefore, my reason for the need to

Vires: Cloak of Dawn/Silent Voice

write on the untold tales of slavery would be supported in such statements as written by men of the past according to the last part of my quotation, which tells us that free men have been captured and forced into slavery.

One would not, as a God-fearing and Bible-believing individual, discuss the untold tales of slavery without referring us to the story of Joseph the son of Jacob as was sold to Egyptian traders, which of course was as a result of hatred from his own very siblings which we all see and understood to be the handiwork of God, and if you don't believe that, then check out the outcome of his brothers' actions against him.

The story of Joseph as it is elaborated in the book of Genesis, the connections between Genesis and Exodus, The Hebrews a handful of people into a large nation. The father and the mother of Joseph been deceived by ill-filled brothers of the other of their sons never knew in a million years that that was the plan of the almighty God to provide for them in times of famine. You could just imagine, the pain Rachel, as a mother must have went through, if she was alive at the time that her son was knowingly sold into slavery by his siblings. Although the Bible did not tell us much about Rachel, So, we may never know but unto everyone's imagination, the pain that woman went through for losing her son which then was tactically told dead by her other sons. You would wonder why all this illustrations? But the fact of the matter is that in every slavery undertaken and experiences if you are a child of God and a God-believing society God has a reason for the slaved and the enslaver. Yes there is always a mission for each and every one of us, although, some carry it out and there are others who execute either way. There are good and evil and some fall on everyone both the good and the ugly, say for instance Judas in the scripture that betrayed Our Lord and

Vires: Cloak of Dawn/Silent Voice

Savior Jesus Christ. Don't you think that that was his mission as a disciple? He did sell his master our Lord and HE was captured but remembers the woe that goes with his action. What I am trying to say is that in every uncomfortable situations we find ourselves_ if truly you read the trend of slavery or history of mankind_ there is absolutely a reason behind it. Blacks were brought from the coast of Africa into Europe for slavery, but see the way they paved for the other African nations and the world at large. Though our forefathers, brothers and sisters, suffered in this country. Today a black man rules the nation and the world because United States of America, as we know it, whether you like it or not, believe it or not and accept it or not, United States of America, is the world leader. This is because our founding fathers obeyed and honored God, and the nation was established under God's rules and commandments. Look back into the story of Joseph in the land of Egypt. The slave became the financial controller of the nation of Egypt. That as a result of Joseph sold into slavery, even his siblings and father later were fed through his agony, torture, loneliness and despair as a slave. So, to everyone, state, nations live every moment as you obey God because what you see as suffering may turn out to be a blessing in disguise, and sometimes the result of a nation's sin and disobedient may result into a dungeon of slavery. So I would advise us to also choose the right part, for there are consequences for every of our undertaken. And may result to a great nation going down the drain as you welcome sin undermining the principles of our founding fathers. A word they say, is enough for the wise.

In our modern generation there are slavery everywhere, and the society seems to look the other way. A hard-working immigrant is prevented benefits because he/she is not a citizen of that

Vires: Cloak of Dawn/Silent Voice

society. They most time are paid under the table with minimal pay per hour. What do you call that? Anyway, hierarchically is better than slavery. At least one is receiving some sort of benefit, unlike our slave fathers and mother who actually contributed to the greatness of this our great nations, America for example, looking at history they went through hell and back, may God bless their souls, but I still believe that God has a reason for their enslavement I would say, but for them and their labor most of the nations would not enjoy what they are enjoying today. Sometime I wonder what we as a race did wrong that our forefathers should go through such unhuman experience from the hands of their fellow men in the name of slavery. The black race should learn to obey and honor God that such punishment of slavery would be a thing of the past. I am not saying verbatim that the black race must have sin against God to have been taken into slavery but who knows and who can tell but we as a race of humanity depends mainly on history and who knows how accurate is the writer of our history because man cannot exist without error and misinformation either by mission or omission. The fact of the matter is that as an African from Nigeria, The truth be told, we rather pay honor to the trees, the land, sea and other imageries than to God Almighty. We should as a race worship the true and the only God instead of all the distractors we consider as gods. Thou shall worship the only true God and Him shall you only serve, for God is a jealous God. So think as you deal and treat your fellow man as though, they are less than a human being. Remember the Bible states that "the earth is the Lord's and they that dwell therein and the fullness thereof"[Psalm 24;1]. Give people the chance to live life to the fullest and stop the slavery that is currently modernized Let freedom reign in every man's life, in every works of life as we live to obey the laws of the land as ordained by our creator. Stop the discriminations and suppressions as this would prevent most abuses that take places in the homes, work places and the community at large. Speak up against such act of slavery if observed as you put yourselves in the enslaved position.

Ponder as you read. Let's make our earth and society at large livable by and for all man. God bless our motherland the "EARTH" as we live by God's directives which is the word of God and there is no ifs and buts about it.

Vires: Cloak of Dawn/Silent Voice

Vote of thanks

This book, Vires / Cloak of Dawn Silent Voice volume 2, would not be written without, first and foremost acknowledging those that were somewhat instrumental in the publication of the first volume.

And those I should say; the almighty God, who gave me the gift to write. Who also made it possible for my migration to one of the greatest countries in our planet earth, which is the United States of America Secondly, my beloved parents, Chief Gad.Walipa.Umajie and Mrs. Selina Ugbe-Umajie. My parents were not just baby bearers but the epitome of love for family and children. What a blessing to be one of their children. Thanks to Joe and Jr., the gift of the womb, my two gorgeous sons, who made my rough life in the United States of America worthwhile. Thank You? I can't say thanks enough for the joy you brought into my life in the mix of the turbulences.

Furthermore, my sincere thanks goes to Ms. Eugenia .B., of Adventist Rehabilitation Hospital of Maryland. At Takoma Park, who was one of the unit secretary's that I was privileged to work with as an agency patient technician staff with Maxim health care in the early 2000. She was the reason why all my thoughts in poetry were written down and saved instead of being trashed. Thereby, I was able to post my works via social media on sites like Poetry.com and Triond.com. I kept my poetry work, because she was the architect behind my realization that my ability to write those thought randomly was truly a gift that I needed to pursue. In one of my moments of thought while standing at her desk. I wrote a poem entitled "GOLD" and gave it to her to read and after she read it, she gave it to the rest of the staff that were around her. Amazed with my gift, she decided to type my work and give me the copy and implore me not to destroy it. She vehemently advised me to keep any future writings of that sort instead of "destroying them." There and then, I promised her that I will keep my writings and never toss them away as I had done previously. I listened and kept Gold and any other poem thereafter.

Furthermore, an RN by the name of Frank Apau, who I worked with at the Adventist Rehabilitation Hospital of Maryland, located at 9909 Medical Center Drive in Rockville, Maryland 20850. While still working as an agency patient technician, " After viewing my freelance write-ups on poetry.com, he advised and encouraged me" to publish my work. He went so far as to make sure, that he gave me a phone number of one of his family members. Who had published a book previously with Xlibris. Which geared me toward discussing to publish my pieces with her further and eventually became a published author in the year 2011.

Also, my thanks goes to the publishing company, Xlibris.com.Though, for years of my poetry.com postings, they have been contacting me about the publication of my book, "though," I never responded to them till I had an encounter with Frank. My warmest heart gratitude is to Mr. and Mrs. David Okonah whom I have known for almost twenty years. They were the individuals God used to lead me to this amazing woman of God that made this publication possible, Mrs. Berth P. Bentlely. Lastly not least, my sincere thanks to the man that made it possible for me to migrate to the United States of

Vires: Cloak of Dawn/Silent Voice

America. If not for my journey to the States, my writing of poetry would not have flourished the way it did. So from the bottom of my heart I say thanks to Elems Ukwu Sr. And for those that I did not acknowledge here like my families and friends, I still say thanks. My greatest thank goes to our Almighty God.

Cry of oppression

The shocks of the invisible shackles,

The pounds of pain that are relentlessly encompassed,

Though pounded on the prudent accelerant,

That the rounded road is branded rocky,

Shoveled to the corner of the concrete,

Whereby the walls are deemed dangerous,

As the rest of the world result to silence,

What point to prove as it appears unnecessary?

Wondering the worth of innocence as it appears dwindling,

What a weapon of despair as it seemed,

Sometimes pushes to temporal insanity,

Thought a few inches away to vengeance,

No, God forbid, Vengeance is mine says the Lord,

Why are there such an awful moments as you wonder,

The popular words of wonders and wounded visible,

Rethinking the echoes of revenge as though eminent,

So it seemed as the wait is relentlessly,

The cry of the oppressed overlooked.

Alone journey

Travelled across the ocean alone,

Journeyed across seas and shiny sea,

Travelled across the blue sky alone very alone,

Oh what an earth hectic heavenly journey!

So alone that the dubious beautiful journey was regretted,

Oh what a lone indeed lone journey!

Immaculate was her intended,

So immaculate as it spills with beautiful smile,

Encouraging were the steps to the beautiful paradise as taught,

Steps embedded with faith hope and dreams,

The zest and zeal to complete the alone journey,

Simple steps resulted in a marathon,

Alone it was to almost the finish line,

At last journey accomplished with smiles unending.

Arrow of love

Shooting as it pierces the heart of a king,

Breaking the barrier between Nations,

Conquers the war between Kingdoms,

It speaks so loud that Heaven becomes her limit,

Like that Between Romeo and Juliet,

It pierces so deeply that the strong man is seen and most times interpreted as weak,

So much so that the African accusatory interpretation views it as Voodoo.

While the open-minded mind views it as an antidote that calms the ragging sea,

For the man on a deserted Island with his love feels fulfilled,

Oh what an arrow that was made for mankind,

Worthy of its creation as every man desires and deserves it,

As a child in a home sees his home as a paradise,

A teenager, without proper guidance, goes far and beyond,

A woman with it bubbles, blossoms socially silky at all times,

While the man with it feels fulfilled at all times, one lives to say till

Vires: Cloak of Dawn/Silent Voice

Death do us part,

The King of the castle blooms as seen very fulfilled,

Oh what an arrow of LOVE!

Live, learn, lean, looking as it is the essence of man's existence

Oh what a soothing pain that comes with

The shot of the "Arrow of Love."

Choices

Oh what a Choice!

The choices we make,

Some worth and sometimes overwhelming,

Our choices somehow and some worth overbearing,

Our choices are never one hundred percent right,

Our right choices sometimes wrong,

Our intended choices sometimes reversed,

Our choices go with our life journey,

Sometimes so detrimental that we appear to sink,

Though few a time our choices pivot us to a glorious end,

Our choices are like a wind that blows,

As the wind blows but sometimes never follows her courses,

Sometimes suiting and other times not,

So, we learn to live with our choices.

Cry for family

Painted is the pain of my past,

Possessed with the poison of pain,

Pronounced is the dagger that lies therein,

Prudent as the pain points,

Printed boldly as bravely tackled,

Though seemed pointless,

The pain is unimaginable,

Oh what a pain! Soaking the better part of me,

Joy short-lived as the pain surmounts,

No joy therein Oh what a cry of wolf!

Immeasurable,

Overwhelming brutally draining,

Oh dear Lord, unto thy feet I lay my pains,

The pain as pointless as it is man-made.

Family apart

Pains as cater potted by the strings of desire,

Pushing to the point of no return,

The pointless painted pain,

Though proving pivoted to be man-made,

Buttresses the surmounted bitter pain,

Probing the joy therein,

Extended the sorrow as lonely moments abound,

Joy lasted for a while but the bitter pain of family,

Far away is beyond the measure of pain,

As the bridge between could not bear such capacity,

Pain of family away surmounts slowly,

Though braving the pain but the tears of family apart
overwhelming,

As prudent is the strength of the pain,

Oh family! The pain and tears for being far is indescribable,

Oh had I KNOWN always come last they say,

As years and life away from you seemed unbearable,

Wishing someday soon it would all be forgotten,

Vires: Cloak of Dawn/Silent Voice

Oh Family, living is meaningless without you.

Help

Having a need needed to be met,

Sometimes to the advantage and the satisfaction of another,

Engaging sometimes in the most daring challenges that the parties involved feel the crunch,

Lifting the load of the other sometimes spiritually physically and emotionally draining,

Pulling and purging the feelings within as it is outrageously sinful, although worth the flesh satisfaction,

As it silences the fleshly insanity,

What a request for help!

As thereafter, the spirit man within agonizes.

Home

Home sweet home,

The once a pretty garden of promise,

Hopes lies within thy shades,

Like the stars in the sky,

Varieties of fruits to a full taste,

So much so that we choose to pluck randomly,

The home garden of Gad and Selina,

Vires: Cloak of Dawn/Silent Voice

Oh what an awesome home!

Daring as though sacred like paradise,

How I miss thee,

Home sweet home,

Life they say is a journey,

So I have journeyed far away from home,

Indeed, there is no place like home,

Left behind was my beautiful home,

My home SWEET HOME in Oshiugbokor.

Vires: Cloak of Dawn/Silent Voice

I am

I am here to honor my creator

I am here to stay

I am as I hear the echo of my laughter

I am as I see my footprints

I am as I see my future

I am as I live in peace

I am as I cry, mourn, and rejoice with others

I am as I care for the young

I am as I contribute to mankind

Yes, I am here to stay

Vires: Cloak of Dawn/Silent Voice

Love

Always and usually mentioned as such a powerful entity,

To a man it is the string that binds us all,

Love, how great are thy hands amongst men?

How mighty and excellent is thy route!

So much so that was rooted by the creator,

As two hearts most times beat as one,

As the one with it feels saturated at all times,

As the life, the world around deemed prettily beautiful,

As the beauty of her joy is depicted in her smiles,

As the touch is warmer than the electric blanket

As the chest is softer than the pillow,

So that the desires and taste of food are farfetched,

Sleeping sometimes less needed as LOVE is imminent,

So beautifully fulfilled as the two hearts always beats as one,

Oh! What a beauty to love and to be loved,

What a machine that not only maintains but services,

The love of man.

Vires: Cloak of Dawn/Silent Voice

The inner joy

My Spirit rejoice,

Rejoice in the nick of time,

As you wake up smelling the sweet spring,

The beautiful sweet aroma of spring as from Roses,

The majestic breeze of God's creation,

Showers of blessings pouring like rain,

Blessings of the springs endowed with sunshine and rainfalls,

Oh what a wonder of spring!

Rejoice for the beauty of Sun and rain as it is bestowed upon us all,

Rejoice and weep no more for all His benefits,

Oh spring forth the dawn of God's glory,

So, I REJOICE for the wake of God's glory SPRING.

A mother's legacy

Mother oh mother!

The lioness amongst Tigers,

The Deborah of our time,

The strength of our strengths,

The watchwoman of our camp,

Oh how time flies!

The reason for motherhood,

The homemaker as well as the caretaker,

Oh our beautiful MOM!

Words are not enough,

Our spiritual emblem,

The motherhood of our dreams,

You truly touched, taught and coached,

Motherhood well displayed and practiced,

Today and forever you will be,

Our wonder woman,

Well done for the life lessons,

Adieu our beloved mother, mentor and heroine,

Vires: Cloak of Dawn/Silent Voice

Goodbye mother till we meet again,

Sleep as the memory lives on.

Mother's love

Love so deep that it is beyond measure,

Love so hot that it is untouchable,

Love so luring that you immerse in it,

Love so captivating that you live to honor,

Love so meticulous that it is without stain,

Love so protective that you dare not tamper,

Love so engulfing that we live to soak in it,

Love so warm that it lasts a lifetime,

Love with unlimited yardstick,

Love with natural wholesomeness,

Love so amazing and seductive,

What a love, Mother's love.

Vires: Cloak of Dawn/Silent Voice

My name

Though she is called a woman,

She calls herself a warmer,

Though she is called a looser,

She calls herself a leader,

Though she is called a mother,

She calls herself a movement,

Though she is called a sister,

She calls herself a sinner,

Though she is a mess,

She calls herself merciful,

Though she is called stubborn,

She calls herself steady,

Though she is called these and more,

She is what she is born to be,

She is a perfect mess to a perfect glory,

The woman on a wondrous mission.

Nine Eleven

Nightmare that came visiting as was realistically proven,

Imposed on us all as the whole wide world stood still as we watched,

None provoked actions of a few Hooligans of our modern days on that fateful day in the name of martyrs what an irony,

Equivalent of practical exhibition of our modern Satanism at its best,

Enveloped in the minds of all as we relive every moment of that fateful day,

LOCKING, RELOADING the evil of man against his fellow man,

Eventually realizing how realistic such evil roams our beautiful globe,

Vindictively affecting us all,

Echoing in the hearts, minds, movements of every Tom and Harry,

Never to be forgotten as we expand to mourn that Fateful Day,

"Nine Eleven"

Our world

So deep high and wide,

So wide that it widens our horizon,

So deep that it drenches as it deepens our determinations,

So high that it propels even the innocents amongst us,

Slowly it begins as it beckons the end,

Our world either molds or breaks us,

So much that it propels us to and fro, up and down the circle,

Divinely it is the totality of us all,

Our world what a divine institution,

The paths unknown but directed by the creator,

Our world what a marvelous intertwined web,

So graciously and marvelous in our sight.

Beauty of love

Oh love!

How beautiful art thou,

The reason we get up in the morning,

The reason we want to live, the reason we bathe,

The reason we smile,

The reason we look out for our neighbors,

The reason we protect our homes,

The reason we labor,

The reason we walk miles with no regrets,

The reason we cry upon seeing our neighbors or friends cry,

Yes indeed we can conquer all things,

Love indeed is the pillar that   holds mankind,

Just like a serial killer would not kill those he LOVES,

Even in their devilish state of mind,

They still feel what they feel for someone,

They actually love,

So I salute thee, Love.

Chained unaware

Oh thou restraining invention!

Created by the mind of the master of illusion,

By the bullies of other creations,

As was invented in the past, present and would be in the future,

Used for the stagnation of their opposition,

Thou art truly a deterrent of God's creation for freedom,

Why, why, chain why?,

Who is thy creator and why indeed,

Why art thou made to deter others?

Chained like a wild dog that is ready to attack,

Why don't you let the wild roam in its territory?

What is the use of her kind if she is in chains?

Why chain a dog that is there only to hunt and provide for her loved ones?

Thy creation would have been appreciated if not vindictive,

Though sometimes necessary for a dangerous specie that poses danger,

But for an animal that just want to roam and enjoy nature,

Vires: Cloak of Dawn/Silent Voice

Thou indeed are not necessary,

As you impede man's creation from exploration.

The Cross

Though I carry my cross,

My cross reflects and affects all around me,

Though I SORROW,

My sorrow reflects and affects all around me,

Though I cry, weep or wail,

It all reflects and affects everyone around me,

Though I rejoice, sing or laugh,

It reflects and affects all around me,

Though upon all the taste of my tears,

It does not reflect or affect those around me,

Because the tears of my weeping can only roll into my mouth,

Just like a mother who has lost a child,

Another mother can empathize,

But truly empathy cannot equate the true pain of the victim,

So I say he that bears the cross,

Knows the weight that goes with it.

The rain pours down on all,

But the appreciation is most different.

Morning glory

My Spirit rejoices,

Wake up with the spring aroma,

Oh what a majestic aroma of God's creation,

Showers of rain upon every creation,

Sun shines as it radiates upon us all,

Thou blessed recipient of all, weep no more,

Thou ought to rejoice in all both great and small blessings,

Do not forget all His benefits,

How deep were the depths of the dungeons?

Why weep for those insignificancies?

Weep no more as thou calculate thine blessings.

There is darkness, but light is eminent at the end of the tunnels,

Like a pregnant women who will not remain pregnant forever,

The night is inevitable, likewise the dawn,

Spring up like the flowers in the spring,

Negotiate no more with Thy bed,

Embrace them all for thy Pilot controls the Ship,

Therefore I say rejoice and embrace the dawn of day.

50

Vires: Cloak of Dawn/Silent Voice

Ekpeye, my motherland

My home, my motherland, the joy of my youth,

How art thou falling?

What was once the beauty of neutrality has become a den of ruin?

We once walked hundreds of miles away from our villages,

Visiting families and friends within and without our motherlands,

Mid-morning and mid-night travelling to market squares in different villages,

We once opened doors and gave rooms to strangers to rest their feet before,

Why are these and more made to be history in this generation?

Why can't we resurrect our once beautiful land? While a child can play around her neighborhood,

Travelling to places with no panics,

Exploring the bushes in search of our natural foods such like snails and others,

Why can't our children taste freedom and security like our fathers provided for us?

What will it take for us to restore peace and order in our land?

Vires: Cloak of Dawn/Silent Voice

Ekpeye, there is nothing worthy of our peace and security,

So I say, come back Peace and Tranquility in my motherland.

Vires: Cloak of Dawn/Silent Voice

Virtuous woman

Oh what a virtue!

She thinks and drools about her family,

She gets up early every day and back to bed with that thought,

Works tirelessly with the thought of her family,

Sleeping, walking, thinking and still dreams of her family,

Like most women, for her young takes abuses,

Though with countless oppositions, still rises up,

She springs up like a flower in her season but in all seasons,

Love undoubted as her strength enormous,

Her vigor beyond measure like unquenchable dreams,

Her faith, hope and charity immeasurable,

Thou art truly a virtuous woman.

Wasted

My long-lasting lust of beauty,

Love unknown as life so daring,

Seen as a drag of day as time flies,

My life my lost my love,

How it all zoomed away in a twinkle of an eye

As I wondered wallowed in the wilderness,

Oh what a beauty of life once lived,

Now flown afar off,

So adored but sinking like a ship in an ocean,

A quick sink of the mighty ship slowly fades away.

Floating somewhere within a deep sea,

The life lust and love once a dream so enticing,

The deep dark ocean of lust,

So she wails for restoration of a life wasted.

Vires: Cloak of Dawn/Silent Voice

Flesh

Oh man that thinks of himself so highly,

Have you thought of how you came to be?

What a wonderful formation of man,

Have you ever imagined the mysteries of your formation?

How about where, and how that surrounds your existence,

How about where and how you will go from here?

Do you sometimes soak on the beauty and the ugliness surrounding you?

Dust we come, Dust shall we all go.

So why don't we live, learn and try to identify the web of our formation.

Though the flesh tend to dictate our moves,

We should not allow the flesh to channel our path,

So, dust your flesh that your return to dust will be Heavenly bound,

Dust as though, today is your last for the purity hereafter.

So unto dust you will return gloriously.

Righteousness

Should we say we are righteous because we believe in God?

Should we say we are totally in tune because we believe in God?

Should we say we are righteous because we believe in God?

Yes we believe in God.

Should that make us righteous indeed?

Oh yeah, Not so quick, after all, we lied, despised, crucified our redeemer.

Numerous ways and several times,

Though we believed the truth is obvious,

The three main requirements are

Hope, Faith and Charity

Charity being Love,

Do we have this one main requirement of us as believers?

Let's ask ourselves,

DO WE HAVE Love?

Love God's way,

Pure love, no strings attached

So, Let's LOVE because if we love,

Vires: Cloak of Dawn/Silent Voice

There will be no lying, deceit, and others,

Just as common in our DAYS

Let us learn to live and LOVE as believers.

Vires: Cloak of Dawn/Silent Voice

Broken

Thou art broken like a broken glass.

How into pieces is thy existence!

Such as thine promises dreams aspirations,

Oh how broken is thine heart like a promised vacation that was unrealistic,

How assorted are thy brokenness?

Destiny they say, stands and pivots one's life outcome,

How come such a brokenness?

The paradise of brokenness into a blessing unknown,

Broken promises as the relationships of our youth,

Broken we were made as aligned with one's neutrality,

So broken as the spears imbedded within us all by the bullies,

The brokenness overwhelming like the cancer of our days,

Indeed very cancerous but healing sometimes imminent,

Oh how broken I am indeed!

Still I STAND because the pioneer,

The architecture of the glass still lives.

Grace, the believer's paved way

Grace is common saving and divine,

Oh what a marvelous entity,

Marvelous in our sight like answered prayers,

A patient recovering from a terminal illness haven told by doctor,

That he has few months to live,

The life of a believer in God Awesome with Grace,

Though we dwindled North South East and West in our FAITH,

Yet Grace abounds for us all;

What a marvelous Grace!

This Awesome entity is available and reachable for all,

All it entails is making the move like taking a sheep to the waters,

All she needs is to drink the available water "Grace of God."

What a glorious gift for mankind!

Why don't you thirst for such a GRACE?

Now available for you and me

Vires: Cloak of Dawn/Silent Voice

Also given by Him who knows the way of life eternity.

Freedom

Oh freedom!

Who is thine architect?

The hope and dream of all man,

The desire of all animals,

The epitome of our liberal minds,

How unrealistic art thou,

Who and what is freedom after all?

The bate of the free world,

Thou unreachable like untouchable flame,

Thine existence exists for so many just for the few,

The wealthy, bullies and for the Prince of this world,

Thou are high above the earth like the sky,

Thou are patterned for the privileged few,

Thou art designed and designated for the very few,

Freedom who and where are thou?

How could thou be when a man running from danger,

Is made to walk miles across border for thy search,

He is locked up, detained, separated from family,

Vires: Cloak of Dawn/Silent Voice

Children dead as a result in search of thou,

Just because he cannot afford thine fame and financial capabilities,

So I ask again who art thou after all,

The reason for man's existence for our beautiful mother Earth.

Vires: Cloak of Dawn/Silent Voice

Purple Peter

Pinky Spooky Peter,

Purple Peter Pinky,

Pinky Purple Peter,

Purple Pinky Peter,

Peter Pinky Purple,

Pooh Spooky Peter,

Spooky Peter Pinky,

Pinky Peter Pooh,

Pooh Pinky Peter as Purple Peter Pinky.

S.H.I.T.H.O.L.E

S—Show casing our world

H—Home with Savagery

I—Integrity with Arrogance

T—Talk of the nations

H—Holding back deemed political politeness

O—Omen of the political minds

L—Lost in the logistics

E—Energizing tool of the wise.

Speaking the truth most times sets you apart,

Sometimes most of us dislike ourselves for being reminded of the truth,

The truth they say would set us free,

Then why do we murmur when the truth is told?

Does it mean that man does not want to be free?

How then do we classify a nation of lawlessness?

A nation where human beings are valued based on their genitalia?

Vires: Cloak of Dawn/Silent Voice

A home, community, society where a female has no say amongst her kind,

A nation where one cannot sleep, wake or walk freely.

A nation where the indigenes escape from to self-slavery abroad.

A nation where the citizens perish at sea escaping their lands,

These are indeed shithole countries.

Shattered dream

In a very few moments dreams turned sour,

Hopes and dreams of the loved,

Promises of party and celebrations,

Informing us about the realities of illusions,

Sometimes appearing tangible, several times so it seemed,

Waking up just to realize is just a dream,

Why can't we all dream dreams that are real,

Some dream dreams others just a nightmare,

What shall we say then, when ones dreams are shattered,

Either by the seen or the unforeseen powers,

We see such obstacles as shattered dreams.

The dream maker brings to pass the real.

Vires: Cloak of Dawn/Silent Voice

Summary

This book in a nutshell is about the vires, the life of us as human in every society.

Man's outlook in life as it starts from our homes, churches, organizations, cultures in our present day societies as it pertains to all other affiliations, the acceptable and the unacceptable norms. The love, strength that is embedded in each and every one of us and the need for everyone to be allowed or given the freedom to express or live their lives just like the man next door. Also the power of love as it starts from the home and extended to the world around us. This in essence is covered in most of my poetry work. If we all should live in peace and unity, we can make this earth a better place for all. Do not encourage hate or evil, speak up against evil when you see one and treat others as you would like to be treated which in essence would birth a stronger community and the world at large. Remembering that we are all passengers passing through this galaxy. Hate no one because they don't belong in your organization or believe the same thing like you do and see no man as less than yourself because they do not come from the tribe you come from or country. Every human being should have the same right like the next, no matter their sex and ethnic backgrounds, as long as they abide to the laws of the land.

The after-Christmas reflection

How many and how much Christmas have you witnessed or observed in your life? Or are you a parent or a child still viewing what the celebration of Christmas is all about? Were you born in a home where the celebration of Christmas was a natural norm I should ask? Or a yearly culture of your community? Or a neighbor, a standby, watching the rituals that go with this great celebration? The greatest or the million-dollar question of this year's Christmas of 2011 is "What are your accomplishments for such a great celebration, as gifts and hugs are shared"? Do you ask yourself is that what Christmas is all about? No, absolutely not. The ultimate question should be, how is my, your and our relationship with the Man in question that is being celebrated?" Jesus Christ the Son of God, of whom we are told in the book of John 3:16, For God so loved the world that He gave His only begotten Son that whosoever believes would not perish but have everlasting life. Are you in line or in tune with Him and His principles? Remember, John 3:16 is commonly recited by all, both practical Christians and none. So, to my fellow celebrant and the world at large, the readers of this book, I would implore you to ponder on this as you read and spread this message of salvation to all mankind as you share your gift and hugs within and out of season of the great Christmas celebration.

CHEERS AND HURRAYS forever as He is and was the only known leader in history that has defeated death and even the grave for mankind.

Vires: Cloak of Dawn/Silent Voice

The cushion of a woman's heart

Her knowledge and acknowledgement of self,

As surrounded by the pillar stronger than life,

Maintained and held by the strongest,

Caressed by the best of the species,

Pampered, possessed by the most of them all,

Admired, cherished by the captain of the ship,

Sailing the Ocean appears nominal,

Piloted by the most experienced of them all,

Sorted, kept and maintained by the warmest,

The heart of humor filled with vigor,

As the longevity of her youth never ceases,

Oh what a heroes as fulfilled in the cushion of her heart,

As saddled from earth unto eternity.

The glory of the Lord

It hovers around us,

It is within this place,

It is within our hearts,

It is within this generation as it was in the past,

It is marvelous in our sight,

It is in His Holy Temple,

It is in our homes and churches,

It is here and now and everywhere,

It would forever be marvelous in our sight,

God's glory couldn't, shouldn't and wouldn't be refuted,

The glory of the Lord!

Truly marvelous in our sight.

Holy Bible

Oh what a Mirror!

What an extreme X-ray,

What a victorious Vine,

What a sensuous severe Sonogram,

What a divine directional Doctor,

What a scientific victorious Visionary,

What an Excellency in efficiency,

What a medium of Mammography,

What a sensation of Sanity,

Perfected Window of wisdom,

Absolute in totality as designed,

Oh what a Wisdom for the wise,

The holy word of God,

The word as we read continually.

Vires: Cloak of Dawn/Silent Voice

The life we live

The root of the tree is significant to the successful growth of the plant and the soil that holds it. The plant cannot water itself, but the nutrients as present in the soil and the water within is a key to the successful germination of the tree as one would presume, but who is the planter? Or should I say, who is the creator of the tree, the soil, the water or the natural nutrients surrounding the tree resulting to the success of the plant as whole? One would not fail to understand that the creator is the originator of everything as stated above.

The grass may appear greener on your end but do not rejoice in mockery of your fellow man because you are placed in a better position in life as you think. Although, so it appears, or seems it does not mean perfection of life but what is success for one man could be seen as a curse for the other. That one begins to wonder is it worth it after all? For instance, a young man born with the golden spoon in his mouth, as presumed by the whole society concerning the home he was born into, is seen as the perfect home by the ordinary eyes but turned out to be untrue due to the result of his future testimonies against his strikingly rich father, whom he finally sent to an early grave as a result of supposedly claimed abuse.

Who would then say the grass is greener in the other side? The creator knows us all and places us all in our various positions in our lives.

Vires: Cloak of Dawn/Silent Voice

The young man or the millionaire's son turned out to be a murderer, serving prison term presently, and his father killed , his mother became a widow suddenly and his older brother is known to be living an isolated life in a desert, not allowing any visitors. What an outcome for the so-called good life.

What is your mission here on earth? How deep have you gone? What path are you following? Are you on the broad or the narrow way? Are you the greedy one or he that empathizes with the neighbors? Are you contented with what you have or the man who has everything but still "wants his neighbors"? Fellow man or you should "look before you leap." We should all know or remember that we are planted here for a purpose and all the nutrients around us are made possible by our creator, although, man sometimes waters his plant. And hopes for a successful season but who is man to decide? Because the outcome of your plant is not solely dependent on the water or how hard you have worked but is destined or approved by the designer of the earth.

The measure of the depth of one's mission could be rocky, but the joy of your rockiness is comforted in your hope and trust in He who creates all the nutrients that enhance the growth of the plant that results in a beautiful tree.

Though, in life so many go about the growth of their plants in different ways for their selfish reasons. But have you asked yourself, Am I, doing it the right way? Is your conscience okay with whatever step you are taking? Do you want to be a millionaire but unprepared for what lies ahead? How deep is your plant? Is it going to bear fruit that is worth consuming or the fruit that shines to Roth? Remember wealth is good, notoriety as well, all the good things life can offer, but the word of wisdom has said, that the fear of God is the beginning of wisdom, So, let us learn how to live this our lives from the word of God.

Whatever you are doing, be sure to do it with all you might with passion, for how much effort you put into your workbe remembered for generations to come either good or bad, So, you decide. The ball is in your court. Though a righteous life is easier said than done but we should not stop trying. The slogan is this; never stop trying to be the best you can be by His Grace.

The loss of innocence

Once then always vivacious idol of all,

Beaming like the sparkling blue sea,

Now wondering the waves as tainted therein,

As the mighty melancholy appeared brandished.

What an arm of faith!

Twisted at the top of the glorious desires.

Winding the truth of vengeance as it dawned deep,

Oh what a pitcher to drink from!

Bitter taste of the furnace of fury,

Wondering the innocuous traits of my youth,

WHAT AN IRONY OF FAITH!

Trapped beneath the Ocean,

Waves and thoughts of swimming daunted,

Therefore resorting to the top arms of Faith,

Oh what a unique union of my innocence.

So daring that was swept under the rogue,

Sweet revenge of my dreams of innocence,

So pronounced pointless pain,

Vires: Cloak of Dawn/Silent Voice

As the outcome of vengeance is redirected,

Oh what a loss of innocence.

Vires: Cloak of Dawn/Silent Voice

The machinery of the 21st century

The great question in one's mind these days should be what is the society turning into? And what is the human species thinking about itself? Should we continue to move north and never return south? And if so what would be the outcome? This I mean when we travel north we would always advance our journey but North is never home but South. How do we as the human species get back home? Remember we are the higher beings created in God's image. Why are we undermining such a great and wonderful portfolio? Are we underestimating our capabilities and abilities? As man, who is endowed with the highest thinking faculties, why are we acting like the less-privileged beasts, who could not have the reasoning abilities even when they do, one can still observe that something is lacking. Imagine a lion feeding on its young and a dog which we consider as man's best friend feeding on its puppies on it's pooh, etc..So, with little said in a very simple and sort of rhetorical way, man should rethink, research himself before taking some degrading animalistic approach to life.

Could we say now that, as a result of freedom, everyone and anything goes? What a society of nonchalant attitude.! What do you think would be the outcome of man's undermining behavior to his creator? What are the consequences? Or Does man think that because our creator is a merciful God, HE WOULD LET EVERYTHING SLIDE? Remember one of the great rules is "To Obey is better than sacrifice" If we don't obey our creator but live a loose, such a life-style that is not worthy of emulation as a

Vires: Cloak of Dawn/Silent Voice

society, what kind of men are we? Do you think that our disobedience would change the anatomical and physiological makeup of man? What a myopic individual is man, thinking because of our choices, the society should just sit and embrace such degrading and unacceptable choices in the name of love and freedom. Remember man was created to go into the world and multiply. Man would be seeking for extinction if we continue to live by the dictates of our flesh, so, man sits and thinks as a man your life choices have no consequences. If every human decides to choose and do whatever they felt like doing, what would become of our planet and society and the human race? Because we do not want to pollute the planet of its oxygen, which was readily made for the living species, despite man's disobedience to GOD our maker. Our society is not obligated to agree with choices that few individuals make for whatever reason, which generally or scientifically I would say is mental deficiencies. Hopefully, you don't overlook this article because the words come with directions and inspirations. Make amends when you still have the time, with great love and admiration for man's souls and the planet earth. If a man's brain is wired to do the abnormal, then cry to your creator to fix it or battle to defeat your demons and don't drag a whole nation to ruins. Sin is sin in all religion, culture and society and no amount of civilization or freedom will change that. This we can all take to the bank.

The path of growth

It is mostly dependent on choices,

Somewhat on associations,

So much on the priorities ahead,

Sort of dependent on the family of birth,

Somewhat on the community and

Circumstances of our birth,

Sometimes surrounded by the speech we make,

Most tuned by the steps we take,

Somewhat and somehow determined by

Both the known and the unknown forces,

Sometimes by men and women associations,

Graciously attainable by the will to grow,

Oh what a path!

The path of growth

The rock

Oh what a rock,

The rock of salvation,

The rock of peace,

The rock of joy,

The rock of mercy,

The rock of freedom,

The rock of grace,

The rock of wisdom,

The rock of victory,

The rock of love,

The rock of healing,

The rock of miracles,

The rock of hope,

The rock of faith,

The rock of life everlasting,

The rock on which Island.

Exciting leaps with gallop

The unique expressions of the human species or the lower animal kingdoms is most times, notable in their patterns of existence by the way they move either by walking or running and their patterns of approach as they walk or run towards their environment.

The earth they say, is spherical but in the literal mind one would say that the earth is filled with gallops as one would observe that the earth is never leveled as we meet with hills and mountains, slopes and what have you but the earth is meaningless without the different species that walk through it.

The question is this, how many gallops on your way and how did you leap through them all or how many on your way have you made leap for joy in this your walk of life. What footprint are you leaving behind on your daily walks? What legacy would you leave behind? Would you walk like Peter of the Holy book, the Good Samaritan or the Martin Luther King of the sixties that advocated peace and equality between all colors or the Adolf Hitler the human massacre?

The interesting legend of the past that I would like to pinpoint is that of the Good Samaritan, Who not only saw a helpless individual but stepped up to help a fellow man that was either bitten to pulp by some act of armed robbery gone wrong or an act of a sadistic individual of his days. He did make sure that this helpless man was properly provided for and given medical attention and also footed the bills. He also made sure to return on his way back to see the progress of this unfortunate victim.

The question is how many have we assisted in our daily walks?

Another legend in the book was the man name Peter, He was not known as a royal man or from the royal blood but just an ordinary fisherman, who abandoned his fishing gear to follow Jesus for His redemptive mission for the human species or the entire human race if only you can accept. The question I would ask is, how is your walk of life? Peter saw a man begging for alms. Peter, having no money looked up to the beggar and stated 'Silver and gold have I none but such as I have, I will give unto thee. In the name of Jesus Christ of Nazareth rise up and walk." What a gift, as the poor beggar jumped up leaping for joy! Who have you left leaping for joy in your daily walk? What legacy are you leaving behind?

Are you the rich traveler who had the compassion and the financial capability to back it up following his actions or are you Peter, who acknowledges his potentials in the authority in the name of Jesus and put it to practice? Or the vicious armed robbers or the beggar" In whatever category you find yourself, you have a role to play in our society at large."

Therefore, are you a politician, a pastor, a healthcare provider, a lawyer, a missionary, a writer, a homemaker, and what have you? You have a role to play and at the end of this life mission, the legacy you leave behind will be your footprint from generation unto generation but there are only two parts in life, either the narrow or the broad way or the good and the ugly just like Martin Luther King or the Adolf Hitler.

Vires: Cloak of Dawn/Silent Voice

Therefore, in your walk on the spherical earth filled with gallops ask yourself this question, whom have I cause to leap for joy today and what legacy am I leaving behind as I circle the globe on daily bases? Reach out and make a mark and stop the bickering and finger pointing and discriminations BECAUSE WE ALL BELONG TO THIS EARTH CONTROLLED BY ONE INDIVIDUAL ALONE.

The twitch of fate

Life is a journey filled with mystery,

The master minder of man's mandatory existence,

Though sometimes appears blink,

As somewhat filled with buckets of hope,

Tentatively nurtured by nature after all,

Most bewildered with the bullets of Fate,

Though bottled as safely delivered by destiny,

Twitching as it may be interpreted by some,

Pressured by the packaged destiny,

What a package of despair,

Swallowed as it seemed,

Oh! What a Twitch of Fate.

Vires: Cloak of Dawn/Silent Voice

The umbrella of beauty

It covers so much as it glows,

It shines so much as it attracts,

It flushes down also outward,

It never retains dirt neither last forever,

Rained, snowed on always dries up,

It protects as it enhances heat in storm,

Movement controlled by handler

Sometimes by wind as the handler holds on,

Upon it all still maintains her spot,

Beautiful to hold as she serves her purposes colorfully,

What a carryon companion,

What a beauty of all seasons!

Vires: Cloak of Dawn/Silent Voice

The unknown stranger

Filled with Zeal and desires journeyed into an unknown
territory

Wondered the true tales of this territory and what lies ahead,

Though the future appeared promising and tantalizing

The journey weighed more than anticipated.

Wondered how optimistic as weariness sets in,

Tried to shake that off as the day begets another

Perturbed not determined to surrender not to the roadblocks

Pursued all rigorously and tentatively,

Desiring and determined for the ultimate,

What a journey that was so much anticipated,

Hoping someday sometime soon the years in wilderness,

Fruitfully will accomplish, accompany it's achievement to full,

As the unknown stranger becomes known who has relentlessly,

Refused to settle for less as the obstacles surmount

As she echoes victory at last even in her sleep.

Dedicated to all immigrants, in every parts "of planet Earth" as
they face restrictions in almost every area just because they were
aliens in a foreign country.

Thou blue sea

The doom of darkness,

Shadow of illusion of the night,

Agent of multiple habitation,

Thou mystery of the ultimate man's survival,

That the wisdom of existence is comparatively fussed,

The light breeze of the ancient existence to modern,

Daunted are the imagination of thy tales,

Thy womb is the wonder of thy creation,

So I ask; where lies thy strength,

Though thou art intimidating yet I rejoice,

Though I swam, strength appeared gone,

I will as I rise to shine like the stars above,

As the stars are watched by the lovers of their existence,

So it is the beauty of my rising as filled with the tales of the
waters,

I rise not to shame the maker but to the obedience of our creator,

So I will, we shall as the blue sea is contained by the maker,

So shall it be the tales of the blue sea,

Vires: Cloak of Dawn/Silent Voice

That is here to stay, pattern as well as living a mark now and forever.

Trailing train

Who amongst the fastest is fast enough to trail the train?

Who amongst the smartest is smart enough to dare?

Who amongst the daredevils is man enough to compete?

Who amongst the vigilante is watchful enough to drag the weary body?

Who amongst the brave is brave enough to boost their ego?

As the Snakes, Pigs, and Man are encamped within the rail for the

Dogs to rescue,

Wondering the effort of man as portrayed by those that dared to compete,

Hopefully man has not and would not lose her birthright as the daredevil of the Trailing Train.

Two-way street

Walking and running on the rough roads

Brings solace in redemption,

How fast could one walk into the redemptive Grace,

What a hope of redemption, as the rough road seems to pierce the soles of the walker,

Who is who to run such a daring race?

Whose running racing most times is drenched with the balls of sweat?

As blocking the views thereafter,

Wondering as doubts sometimes creeps in,

Why the doubts as it is impeccably determined,

That man's way of life is a two-way street.

Vires: Cloak of Dawn/Silent Voice

USA election 2016

Oh America!

How art thy mighty falling?

Mirror of the multicultural,

How art thou falling?

Immaculateness of emasculation,

How art thou falling?

Redemption of reduction,

How art thou falling?

Integration of interjection,

How art thou falling?

Condom of amalgamation,

How art thou falling?

Testament of the unknown testimony,

How art thou falling?

Election of 2016,

Thou indeed is the irony of once a free world,

How art thou falling?

The true testament of our world unknown.

Vires: Cloak of Dawn/Silent Voice

Vivacious

The road is broad that seemed narrow,

Smooth slick and slippery,

Though I long to soak and walk on it,

Sometimes wonder if at all,

Most times desire to walk,

Wonder how far and why without a limb,

Wonder if the growth of a limb if possible,

Then wonder again how possible without a means,

How could one without a limb walk or run?

Yes an artificial limb is possible but without a means,

Once there was a dream very great,

Most questionable a walk without a limb,

As beautiful as it flowed the lack of limb,

As the thought of walking becomes slim

Vires: Cloak of Dawn/Silent Voice

Warring flesh

Wakes up to meeting her need,

Selfishly desiring and demanding to every impurity,

Thereby rattling to her unquenchable desires,

She rolls as she rotates intensively,

Nutty was her demands in high velocity,

Overly walking toward domination of the SOUL,

Flooded as it flows with numerous sediments,

As she leaves the soul longing for air,

As most often executes the venom within,

Thereby shattering the joyful soul,

As she constantly drowns in the ocean of sin,

Battering the quest for a fruitful redemption,

Oh flesh what are thy components?

Dust art thou taken and thus shall thou return.

Will

Willing to wallow in the will of wheat,

Wondering the width of the will within,

Watering the windmill within our wings,

Words of wisdom winning within,

Worth the wait as wings almost weathers,

Wondering the watch of wanton,

Windy wicked watch it seemed,

Walked to wait for the wicked watch,

Warning as warm as woes unpredicted,

Wearing the winter coat of warmth,

As though depicted by the warring Lord,

What a wicked will to watch!

Wonders of the mind

Sleeping sensations simultaneously,

Mating match magical,

Cloche in cruelty visible,

Hiking slightly holy,

Crushes and crashes inevitable,

Flattered flattened as left for dead,

Buried beneath the rubbles,

Screamed and shouted to safety,

Suddenly stood to stroll,

Surrounded by surprised onlookers,

Trailer trapped upon,

Immaculately emerged therein,

As suddenly soothes for real,

What a wonder of the mind!